The Big Bear Nightmare

Pigs CAN fly!

Kweeeeeeeeeeeeeeeeeeeeeeep!

When the Alarm Squeal sounds it must
be a job for Captain Peter Porker and
the PIGS IN PLANES!

Paul Cooper is from Manchester.
He now lives in Cambridge with
his wife and two daughters.

Read these high-flying adventures
about the Pigs in Planes:

PIGS IN PLANES: THE CHICKEN EGG-SPLOSION

PIGS IN PLANES: THE SHARK BITES BACK

PIGS IN PLANES: THE BIG BAAD SHEEP

PIGS IN PLANES: THE MEGA MONKEY MYSTERY

PIGS IN PLANES: THE CAMEL'S HUMP OF DOOM

PIGS IN PLANES: THE BIG BEAR NIGHTMARE

The Big Bear Nightmare

PAUL COOPER

Illustrated by Trevor Dunton

PUFFIN

PUFFIN BOOKS

Published by the Penguin Group
Penguin Books Ltd, 80 Strand, London WC2R 0RL, England
Penguin Group (USA) Inc., 375 Hudson Street, New York, New York 10014, USA
Penguin Group (Canada), 90 Eglinton Avenue East, Suite 700, Toronto, Ontario, Canada M4P 2Y3
(a division of Pearson Penguin Canada Inc.)
Penguin Ireland, 25 St Stephen's Green, Dublin 2, Ireland (a division of Penguin Books Ltd)
Penguin Group (Australia), 250 Camberwell Road, Camberwell, Victoria 3124, Australia
(a division of Pearson Australia Group Pty Ltd)
Penguin Books India Pvt Ltd, 11 Community Centre, Panchsheel Park, New Delhi – 110 017, India
Penguin Group (NZ), 67 Apollo Drive, Rosedale, North Shore 0632, New Zealand
(a division of Pearson New Zealand Ltd)
Penguin Books (South Africa) (Pty) Ltd, 24 Sturdee Avenue, Rosebank, Johannesburg 2196, South Africa

Penguin Books Ltd, Registered Offices: 80 Strand, London WC2R 0RL, England

puffinbooks.com

First published 2011
001 – 10 9 8 7 6 5 4 3 2 1

Text copyright © Paul Cooper, 2011
Illustrations copyright © Trevor Dunton, 2011
All rights reserved

The moral right of the author and illustrator has been asserted

Set in Bembo Infant
Made and printed in England by Clays Ltd, St Ives plc

British Library Cataloguing in Publication Data
A CIP catalogue record for this book is available from the British Library

ISBN: 978-0-141-33211-6

www.greenpenguin.co.uk

For Paul Shipton, my mentor

MEET THE CREW

TAMMY SNUFFLES,

Mechanic

BRIAN TROTTER,

Medical Officer

CURLY McHOGLET,

Trainee

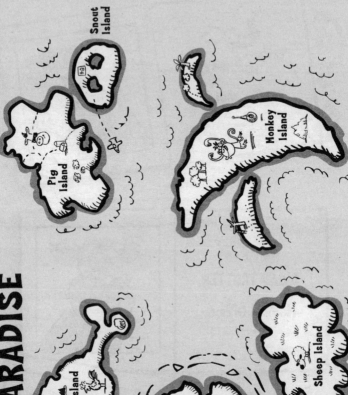

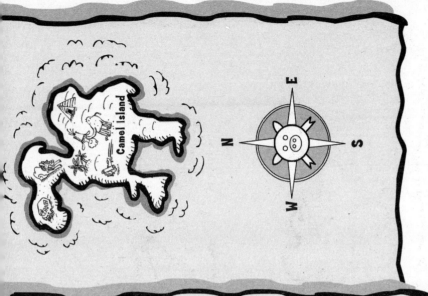

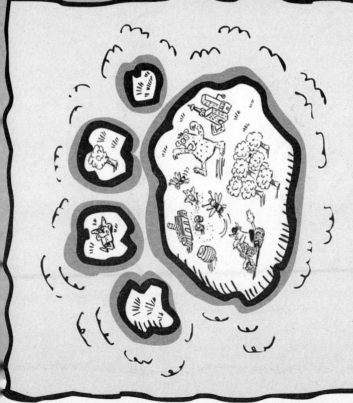

BEAR ISLAND

CHAPTER 1:

The Bear Facts

Captain Peter Porker couldn't help noticing something different about Wing Commander Oinks-Gruntington this morning.

'Er, why's Peregrine wearing a pink baseball cap that says *No. 1 POP PRINCESS*?' he asked Lola Penn.

The PiPs radio operator grinned. 'Do you like it? I put it there!'

'It's a bit small for his huge head,' said Pete.

Peregrine let out a long, strange noise – a snore! Pete went closer. 'He's asleep!' he

gasped. 'With one eye open!'

Lola nodded. 'Cool, isn't it? He's been having trouble falling asleep at night lately, so he's taken to having naps at his desk. He thinks I don't notice!'

Pete crossed his arms and tried to look disapproving. 'So your reaction is to put silly pink hats on his head?'

'That is *so* not true!' huffed Lola. 'I put silly hats of *all* different colours on his head.

Look!' She pulled out her mobile phone and began scrolling through the pictures. It looked like the world's worst hat catalogue.

'And now I can sit back and relax,' Lola beamed. She picked up the latest copy of her favourite magazine *Sizzle!*

Two seconds later there was a BEEP! from the radio.

'WHAT?' sputtered Peregrine, waking up. 'Where am I?'

'Morning, Peregrine,' said Pete.

Lola grabbed the radio microphone. Now her voice was serious and professional: 'You have reached the Pigs in Planes emergency service. What are your inter-species rescue needs?'

The voice on the line was very quiet.

'What's that?' said Lola. 'Something about bears?' She leaned in closer. '*Where've* they gone? You'll have to speak up, sir – or, indeed, madam.'

Lola scrunched up her face with effort. 'What did you say? "Bare bottom"?'

'Must be a prank call,' huffed Peregrine, 'like that time someone called and said all the football boots had been stolen on Snake Island!'

'Shhh, Peregrine!' snapped Lola.

The caller mumbled a few more words and then the line went dead.

Pete's gut instinct was telling him that this might be a genuine call. 'Why don't you just check Bear Island online?' he asked Lola.

The radio operator jumped on to the computer and quickly pulled up a webcam shot from the capital of Bear Island, Ursalona. It showed the main square in the city centre.

'Well, everything looks nice and peaceful there,' commented Peregrine.

But Pete knew better. 'This is a *live* shot, and it's rush hour.'

Lola understood what he meant. 'Of course! There should be bears everywhere – going to work, going to the shops. So where *are* they all?'

Lola clicked to another webcam set up in a different part of the city. Then she clicked to another, and another. It was the same story for all of them. There didn't seem to be

any bears at all on Bear Island. Whoever the caller had been, it seemed they were right – the bears were gone!

Peregrine gave a determined nod, still unaware of his pink Pop Princess cap. This was a job for the Pigs in Planes.

Lola reached out and pressed the Code Pink emergency button. The Alarm Squeal sounded all around the base:

KWWWEEEEEEEEEEEEEEEEEEEP!

The PiPs were going to Bear Island!

As the SkyHog jets zoomed north, the team soon learned that Lola couldn't give any detailed information about the mission. She didn't know who the caller was, or even what the problem was exactly.

'All we've got are the bare facts,' said Pete over the radio, 'which is that there don't seem to be any bears around.'

'Maybe today's the day the teddy

bears have their picnic?' suggested Curly
McHoglet helpfully. Yet to earn his wings,
the trainee was still flying with Pete, as
usual.

'I wish I could have a picnic,' chipped in
Tammy Snuffles, the PiPs mechanic. 'I'm
starving.' Luckily, she had stashed a few bags
of crisps under her jet's console . . . and an
apple pie . . . and a pizza . . . OK, two pizzas.

'Do we know which part of the island
the call came from?' asked Brian Trotter, the
team's medical officer.

'It came from just north of the capital,
Ursalona,' answered Pete. 'There's a place
there called "Bear Bottom Farm" – Lola
thinks the caller might have been trying
to say something about it. But I want to
check out the city centre first and see what's
happening – or *not* happening – there.'

Soon they were flying over the heavy
forests of the island.

'I can see Ursalona up ahead!' cried Tammy, through a mouthful of crisps.

Usually it was tricky landing the SkyHogs in a busy city, but Ursalona was not busy today. Its streets were completely empty.

'I can't see any bears in the streets and I can't see any traffic on the roads,' said Tammy, spraying crumbs of pie crust. 'The place is completely deserted.'

They landed the jets right in the middle of a huge shopping precinct. All the shops were closed, and there wasn't a shopper in sight. The PiPs got out of their planes and

wandered to the side of a four-lane road that ran past the precinct; it had precisely *zero* traffic on it.

'Looks like rush hour has ended,' said Curly.

'Yeah, about three years ago,' said Tammy, taking a last bite of pizza.

Brian turned slowly to take in every view of the bearless city around them. 'Can you hear that?'

Pete cocked an ear. 'No.'

'Exactly!' said the medical officer. 'There's no background noise at all – no traffic, no pawsteps, no TVs or radios. What you can't

hear is the sound of complete and utter silence!'

'Do you know what this is a bit like?' said Curly nervously. 'That science fiction film *The Omega Pig*! It's about the last pig left in the entire world, and he wanders around a deserted city all alone, just like this.'

'And what happens to him?' asked Tammy.

Curly blinked. 'He . . . er . . . gets eaten by giant radioactive spiders that live in the sewers.'

Pete grinned. 'OK, good safety reminder there – everybody keep away from giant mutant spiders. Thanks for that, Curly.' The captain pulled a city map from his pocket. 'We'll cover more ground if we split up. Tammy? You and Curly, search the city centre. Look for anybody who can tell us what's going on. Brian, you're with me – we're going north of the city, to see if we can track down our mystery caller.'

Tammy and Curly started towards the city centre. 'What should we do if we spot someone?' the young trainee called to Pete.

The PiPs captain answered over his shoulder. 'If it's a bear, ask where everyone else is . . . If it's a giant radioactive spider?' He shrugged. 'Better run, I suppose.'

CHAPTER 2:

The Sound of the Underground

Tammy and Curly made their way through deserted streets. Tall buildings towered all around them, but still they saw no sign of life. There was no sound but the clack of their trotters on the pavement.

'I don't like this,' murmured Tammy. 'It's like my cousin Joel ... too quiet and creepy.'

'Hey, I bet your voice echoes if you shout,' said Curly eagerly. He cupped both trotters around his mouth and shouted:

'OINK!'

'OINK!' bounced back the faint echoing reply.

Curly grinned. 'See?'
He shouted again:

'HELLO-OOO!'

'HELLO-OOO!'

'HOW ARE YOU-
OOOO?'

'OK-AYYYYYY!'

The two pigs froze.

'That wasn't an echo,'
gasped Tammy. 'That was an
answer.'

They charged forward
to see where the voice had
come from. As they rounded
a corner, they could see a
small figure moving in the
distance. It was hard to tell
from this far, but it looked
like a little bear cub walking
towards to a sign for the
city's Underground system.

'HEY, YOU!' shouted Tammy.

The little bear looked up and saw two strange, uniformed pigs in the distance running towards him. He didn't seem to like this much, and so he pelted down the steps that led below street level.

'WAIT!' shouted Tammy.

But it was too late. By the time the two pigs reached the Underground entrance, the only living bear they'd spotted in the entire city so far was gone.

'Shall we radio Pete?' asked Curly.

Tammy shook her head. 'Let's see if we can find that cub first. Lola said the person on the radio sounded odd – maybe it was a little kid who made the emergency call?'

The two pigs followed the steps down into the Underground system. The little cub was nowhere to be seen. They continued to follow the tunnel down.

'What's that noise?' asked Curly. 'It's not

your tummy, is it, Tammy?'

This was a reasonable question – the sound was a strange rumble, and Tammy's tummy usually produced one of these half an hour or so after her last meal.

But the mechanic shook her head. 'That's not me – I only had a light snack on the flight over.'

As the PiPs continued along the tunnel, the rumbling became louder. Finally they came to a large entranceway and discovered what was making the noise.

The entrance led into a huge underground cave. Only the dim light of several EXIT signs saved the place from total darkness. Tammy and Curly stood on a steel walkway and looked out on what appeared to be an underground sea of dark fur. It was *bears*, hundreds and hundreds of them, all fast asleep. The rumbling noise was the sound of lots and lots of combined snores.

'What's –' Curly began, but Tammy
clapped a trotter over his snout.

'Shhh!'

Curly dropped his voice. 'What's going on?'

Tammy waved an arm to indicate the
huge cave. 'There are lots of these caves
on Bear Island,' she explained quietly.
'It's where the bears hibernate during the
winter . . .' She scratched her head. 'So the

bears haven't *disappeared*, they're just all hibernating. But why are they hibernating *now*? It doesn't make sense. It isn't winter – it's warm outside.'

'No probs,' said the trainee sunnily. 'I'll just wake one of them up and ask what the problem is. Easy-peasy!' He started down the steel steps to the cave floor.

Tammy flew after him. 'Stop!' she hissed, grabbing his arm just as he reached the bottom step. 'Didn't they teach you *anything* at school? The top three most important safety rules in life are these . . .' Tammy counted them off:

'One: Never set off fireworks next door to a dynamite factory.

'Two: Never press a big red button labelled DANGER, DO NOT PRESS.

'And three: Never – *ever* – attempt to wake up a hibernating bear.'

'Why not?' Curly blinked innocently.

'Because if you wake a bear up too suddenly,' said Tammy, 'there's a few minutes when it doesn't know where it is or what's going on. It can go into a bit of a rage, and trust me – you don't want to be near a bear in a rage.'

Curly looked down now at the huge sleeping bear in front of him. Its powerful arms ended in the sharpest-looking claws he'd ever seen. He'd heard that a bear's claws were sharp enough to slice open a tin of tomatoes. Curly didn't want to see that – he didn't even like tomatoes much.

The two pigs took a careful step backwards on to the staircase. But then they spotted movement on the far side of the

cave. It was the same chubby little bear cub.
They could see now that he was only a
few years old; he wore shorts and carried
a stuffed teddy bear toy in one paw. He was
pushing at one of the sleeping bears, but it
just went on snoozing.

Not daring to shout out, the pigs could
only watch as the cub gave up and started
towards one of the exits on the far side.
Carefully Tammy and Curly began to
thread their way after him through the mass
of slumbering bears.

'Don't step on anyone's fur,' whispered
Tammy. She risked a quiet 'Psssst!' to attract
the cub's attention. 'PSSST!'

Finally the cub did look back. It paused

just long enough to stick its tongue out at the two pigs, and then it scurried to the exit even faster.

'Come on!' hissed Tammy. 'We can't let him get away!'

Curly sped up. Instantly, he tripped on an outstretched furry leg.

Luckily, there was something to break his fall – a large sleeping bear. It didn't wake up, but it swung one gigantic paw over and clamped it around Curly. Still sleeping, the bear hugged the pig closer to it, as if the PiPs trainee was a large stuffed toy or an amusingly shaped hot-water bottle.

Tammy looked down at them. 'There's no time to mess about,' she whispered urgently. 'Come on!'

Curly tried to slide out from under the tree-trunk-sized arm, but the bear just tightened its grip and let out a low growl. Curly wasn't going anywhere in a hurry.

CHAPTER 3:

Everybody do the Brian!

Pete and Brian landed SkyHog 1 near
a large billboard in front of a wire-mesh
fence. The picture on it showed a happy
bear farmer in bib-overalls and a straw
hat. He was holding up a jar of honey next
to a smiling bee. The words said BEAR
BOTTOM HONEY FARM.

Pete sniggered, as he set about climbing
over the fence.

'Why are you laughing?' asked Brian.

'Well, it sounds like "bare bottom", doesn't
it?'

'Yes. And?'

'Well . . . bare bottoms are *funny*.'

'Not to me.' Brian pushed his glasses up his snout and started climbing the fence, too. 'As a matter of fact, I've heard of this place,' he said. 'It's quite interesting, actually – this farm was taken over by the biggest food company on Bear Island, Sweetie Foods. It was in the news because some bears were afraid the company would get rid of the traditional methods of making honey. And so . . .'

Pete honestly *tried* to listen, but sometimes Brian saying the words 'It's quite interesting, actually' acted like an OFF switch on his brain. He watched a little bee pull away from a flower and weave its way through the trees. He could hear a droning sound, and it wasn't just Brian's voice.

Following the bee's wobbly path, Pete cleared the trees and stopped. In front of him, there were hundreds and hundreds

of wooden beehives, all packed together and lined up in rows. Millions of bees were buzzing around, going into or out of their hives. Behind them there was a huge factory of some kind.

'That doesn't look much like the picture on the billboard,' said Pete.

'It must be the honey production plant Sweetie Foods built,' said Brian. He started towards the big ugly building. 'Come on. The bees won't sting us if we don't go near the hives.'

As they made their way towards the big factory, Brian continued, 'As I was saying, honey is quite interesting, actually . . .' (Pete sighed.) 'Bees can tell the rest of their hive where the nectar is by doing a dance. Would you like me to show you?'

'No!' cried Pete.

'Oh, OK . . . Anyway, the bees collect nectar from flowers and bring it back to the hive.'

Pete paused. 'Hold on, Bri – *how* exactly do they bring the nectar back? I don't exactly see any of them holding little buckets . . .'

'They carry it in their stomachs, of course,' said Brian.

Pete was starting to get a weird feeling about this. 'And then what?'

'They regurgitate it back in the hive, of course, before thickening it up in honeycombs.'

'They SICK it back up?' Pete could hardly believe this. 'So when we eat honey on our toast, we're actually eating *extra-thick bee sick*? Why don't they ever put *that* on the label?'

'Um, well . . .' Before he could give a more detailed answer, Brian realized some of the bees were following them. As they passed each wooden hive, more bees joined the little cloud of buzzing insects tracking them.

The buzzing was getting louder and the cloud of bees were coming closer and closer. Every so often one or two braver bees broke away from the main group and shot past the two pigs. It seemed to be only a matter of time before they started stinging.

'Look!' cried Pete. They had come to a pick-up truck. 'There are a couple of beekeeper's outfits here!'

The two pigs quickly pulled on the baggy protective suits and then clamped the broad hats with netting on their heads. They were

just in time – not because of the bees, but because, a moment later, a door in one of the factory's outbuildings opened and two bears ambled out, one of them pushing a small handcart. They wore beekeeper's suits, too, but with their heads uncovered.

They shambled up to the nearest row of hives and began to lift the lids. The PiPs watched as one bear pulled out rectangular wooden frames filled with honey, and loaded them on to the second bear's cart.

'That's how they collect the honey,' whispered Brian.

As the bears neared the two PiPs, they nodded hello.

'All right?' said one bear gruffly.

Pete nodded back. These bears must think that he and Brian were just fellow workers. He was about to throw the dark netting back and ask where all the other bears on the island were, when one of the bears said to his mate, 'Be careful with that honey. Don't want to disappear like all them others on the island.'

The other bear grunted. 'That's not how it works, mate.'

As soon as he heard these words, Pete dropped his trotters from the netting covering his face. Something strange was going on here, but his gut instinct told him that these two workers wouldn't have any answers for them; he and Brian needed to get inside for a proper look round.

He became aware that the two bears were staring. 'Are you two new here or sumfink?' said one.

Pete made his voice go as deep and bearlike as it could. 'Yeah, we're working . . .' He pointed to a distant row of hives. '. . . over there. Right, Bri?'

'YEEEEE!' wailed Brian in a high voice.

It sounded like the cry of a Kung Poo master in combat, but the real reason for Brian's squeal was that one of the bees had made its way into his beekeeper suit before he'd zipped it up. Now it was buzzing around angrily as it tried to escape from this strange, dark prison.

Brian began to hop and jump around, shooting his arms and legs out in weird jerky motions as he attempted not to get stung.

The two bears just watched. 'Is your mate OK?' one asked.

'Yeah, he's . . . doing a new dance,' said Pete. 'It was all the rage in Ursalona . . . you know, before everyone disappeared. Everyone wanted to "do the Brian"!'

The bears didn't seem convinced, so Pete began to copy the medic's odd jerky motions himself.

'Shouldn't you both be working, not dancing?' grunted one of the bears. 'Mr Sweetie doesn't like bears slacking off during work hours.'

'That reminds me!' cried Pete, still doing

'the Brian'. 'There's something we have to tell Mr Sweetie! Come on, Bri – this way!'

The two bears just watched silently as this strange little pair in full beekeeper outfits did their dance all the way to the outbuilding door.

CHAPTER 4:

Hairy Bikers

In the giant cave under the city, the sleeping
bear continued to hug Curly to its massive
chest.

'Do you . . . know any . . . lullabies?'
Curly gasped to Tammy, thinking that the
bear might relax its grip a little if it heard
something nice and restful.

Tammy just shook her head, so Curly did
his best to sing, even though he was now a
dark shade of purple:

'*Rock-a-bye piggy . . . there in your sty.*'

This didn't have much of a soothing
effect. The bear growled louder and

squeezed Curly even tighter. The young pig
looked as if his head might go POP! soon.

Curly tried again: '*Good night, little piggy
. . . asleep in the mud!*'

This seemed to anger the sleeping bear
even more. It was showing its teeth now and
shifting restlessly. Curly looked as if he could
hardly breathe now; there was no chance he
could attempt another lullaby, and Tammy
didn't seem to know any at all.

Suddenly the mechanic flashed a smile.

She started singing something much peppier:

'*You put your right arm in, your right arm out, your right arm in and you shake it all about!*'

The sleeping bear lifted its free arm and shook the lethal-looking claws on the end in time to the song. Several of the other bears within earshot did the same.

Tammy continued singing:

'*You put your left arm in, your left arm . . .*'

As soon as the bear raised the arm holding Curly and shook it all about, the pig wriggled out and leapt to his trotters. He was free! As they made their way to the exit, Tammy continued to sing the chorus of the song quietly:

'*You do the hokey-cokey and you turn around.*'

Curly knew this song well because his nan had always sung it to him.

'*That's what it's all about,*' sang the mechanic gently.

'OY!' shouted Curly, as he had always done at this bit of the song.

At this sudden noise, the snores of the sleeping bears around them turned to angry restless snarls, but by now the pigs had reached the metal staircase and were racing back up towards street level.

They emerged in a different part of the city. This street had buildings on one side and the beginning of thick woods on the other. Once again there was no sign of the bear cub.

Curly stood in the empty road. 'Why are there woods right here in the city?'

'Bears love the woods,' explained Tammy. 'They like to be near them even in the city. They enjoy roaming and eating berries. Most bears even prefer to go to the loo in the woods rather than indoors.' She reached for her radio. 'We'd better call Pete.'

But Curly cocked his head. 'Wait, Tammy!

What's that noise?'

Tammy could hear it, too – Ursalona was silent no more. The silence was broken by the far-off roar of engines. Well, at least it started out as a far-off roar, but it quickly grew louder and louder.

'What IS it?' asked Curly.

Tammy knew. 'Motorbikes,' she said. 'Lots of them.' She grabbed Curly by the wrist. 'I don't think we should be standing in the middle of the road – or even by the side of the road, come to think of it.'

She ran behind the nearest trees, pulling Curly with her. Moments later the front-runner of the big bikes roared round the corner. It was a huge black machine with chopper handlebars and flames spray-painted on the petrol tank.

'Nice wheels,' murmured Tammy.

The enormous grizzly bear riding this motorbike wore a denim jacket with the sleeves ripped off to show his gigantic hairy arms. On his feet were the biggest motorbike boots Curly had ever seen, and on his huge shaggy head he sported an immense Viking helmet.

All in all, he looked like one tough, mean biker bear, and the other biker bears that appeared round the corner looked every bit as tough – if not tougher.

'Why are *they* awake?' Curly asked. 'Shall we flag them down and see if they know what's going on?'

'No!' Tammy's trotter fell on the young pig's shoulder. 'Did you see the name on the back of their jackets?'

Curly nodded. 'The Gruesome Grizzlies.'

'The GGs are the meanest, toughest, most dangerous gang of grizzly bikers on Bear Island,' said Tammy. 'I've heard rumours they pull the heads off anyone who annoys them. You do NOT want to go asking them questions.'

The last of the bikers was riding by now, and the roar of the engines was beginning to fade.

'But what about that poor little cub?' Curly asked, his eyes wide with alarm. 'We can't let him fall into the clutches of a nasty gang of grizzly bikers, can we?'

'No,' agreed Tammy. 'Which means that

right now we have to go into these woods.'

'Why?'

Tammy pointed to a spot a little way into the forest. There, on the ground, lay the little battered teddy bear that the cub had been carrying.

CHAPTER 5:

Going on a Bear Hunt

Pete and Brian hurried through the metal doors into a large loading area. Several bears in overalls were stacking hundreds of the honeycomb-filled frames from the beehives on to a conveyor belt. The two pigs kept their beekeeper disguises on and nobody questioned them as they headed towards the factory floor.

This place was alive with the rattle and hum of machinery. However, there did not seem to be any bears working here. It was all fully automated.

Pete pulled the netting of his beekeeper's

helmet back. 'That's better,' he said. 'Now I won't bump into things quite so much.'

'Perhaps if you'd taken your sunglasses off?' suggested Brian.

'Right, good one!' Pete smiled, not realizing that this hadn't been a joke.

Meanwhile, Brian was studying the machines around them.

'Industrial honey production is quite interesting, actually,' he began. He pointed to the conveyor belt carrying all the honey-filled frames from the loading bay. They were moving towards a machine with a razor-sharp chopping blade.

'That slices the beeswax away so they can get at the honey inside,' Brian explained.

'Really?' mumbled Pete. In truth, he was only half-listening. He was also gazing at his own reflection in one of the shiny metal machines and thinking that he was looking particularly fine today.

Brian pointed at another machine, a large metal drum. 'Then that machine spins the frames around really fast to get the honey out,' he explained.

'Really?' Pete turned his head to see how his hair looked from a different angle. The word *perfection* popped into his head.

'And then the honey drains off

into that great big vat,' Brian was saying. 'But here's what I don't understand. The honey is usually bottled after that, but in this place it gets pumped through *another* machine into this second big vat. So my question is – what do they do to the honey between Vat 1 and Vat 2?' Brian dipped his trotter into the second vat and tasted the honey. 'Seems pretty normal,' he said. 'What do you think, Pete?'

'I think it was a good idea upgrading to that new extra-hold hair gel,' Pete answered. When he realized Brian was giving him an odd look, he pulled his eyes away from his reflection. 'Er, sorry . . . what was the question, Bri?'

In the stretch of inner-city woodland, Curly looked down at the old toy teddy bear in his trotter. It gazed back up at him with its single glass eye.

'I had a teddy when I was little,' Curly said. 'His name was Mr Ploppy.'

'Why did you call it "Mr Ploppy"?'

Curly reddened. 'I don't want to talk about it.' He quickly changed the subject. 'Didn't you use to have a teddy bear, Tammy?'

'No,' the mechanic said quickly. Her tone

made it clear she didn't want to discuss the matter further, either. She was examining the ground ahead. She pointed now at a faint line of little pawprints. 'This way.' The two pigs plunged into the woods.

'Hey, you know what this reminds me of?' asked Curly. 'There was a song we used to sing at piglet camp, "Going on a Bear Hunt". Do you know it?'

Tammy just shook her head, and Curly wondered why she didn't seem to know any of the things that had been big parts of his own childhood. 'I'll teach you!' he cried. 'I'll sing one line and you just sing it back at me.' Still running, he cleared his throat and began to sing:

'We're going on a bear hunt.'

Tammy felt silly but, not wanting to dampen the young pig's spirits, she sang the line back: 'We're going on a bear hunt.'

'I'm not afraid,' sang Curly.

'I'm not afraid.'

Suddenly Curly noticed something clinging to his leg. 'WAH!' he screamed. 'WAAH! A big fat BUG!'

Tammy was confused – what sort of songs had Curly learnt as a piglet? – but she did her best to copy the note of panic in the trainee's voice:

'WAH! WAAH! A big fat BUG!' she chanted.

'Get it off me! Get it off!' wailed Curly, flapping his trotters about and running in circles.

Tammy shrugged. He hadn't said anything about dance moves, but if she was going to do this, she may as well do it properly. *'Get it off me, get it off!'* she cried, flapping her own trotters wildly, just like Curly.

'This isn't part of the song!' the young pig cried. The mystery bug on his leg decided to

fly off and look for somewhere a bit quieter.

'This isn't part –' Tammy paused. 'Oh . . . I see.'

The two pigs ran on, swishing their way through some long grass and then deeper into the woods. Curly continued to hum the same campfire song under his breath. Soon the path narrowed until they had to go single file.

Suddenly, Curly stopped: there, in front of them, was a puddle of mud. Tammy eyed it over the trainee's shoulder.

'Better go round that,' she commented.

'No!' cried Curly. 'It's just like in that Bear Hunt song I told you about!' He began to sing again:

'Came to some mud – sticky, icky mud! Can't go ROUND it! . . . Can't go UNDER it! . . . Got to go THROUGH it!'

As he sang the final line, he marched forward into the squelchy mud. Then he stopped and looked down.

'Erm, this mud is a bit stinky,' he said.

'That's because it isn't mud, Curly.'

Curly wrinkled his snout. 'What is it then?'

The PiPs mechanic sighed. 'Remember when I told you what bears do in the woods?'

'That they like to roam and eat berries?'

'No . . .' said Tammy. 'The *other* thing. What they do AFTER they've eaten the berries.'

Understanding hit Curly.

'Uh-oh.'

CHAPTER 6:

Hello, Sweetie

On the other side of the factory floor, there was a corridor with several offices dotted along it. Pete peeked into each one. 'This looks like the sort of place we'll find some answers,' he said.

Brian followed the captain into a large meeting room. There was a long table in the middle, with a little honey pot set in front of each leather chair. Each pot had a name label on it – *Rupert*, *Winnie*, and so on. One pot was much bigger than all the others – it bore the name MR SWEETIE.

On the wall above the fireplace there was

a portrait of a grumpy-looking bear in a pinstriped business suit.

'That's Mr Sweetie, the head of the company,' said Brian.

'He doesn't look very cuddly,' said Pete.

'He isn't.' Brian pointed at the company

SWEETIE BY NAME
NOT BY NATURE

motto under the portrait: SWEETIE BY
NAME, NOT BY NATURE.

The medic stifled a yawn with the back of
his trotter.

'This mission isn't boring you, is it?' asked
Pete.

'Sorry!' said Brian, trying to shake off his
sleepiness. 'I'm just feeling suddenly very tired.'

Pete frowned. Then he said, 'Here's
something that will wake you up! I can hear
footsteps in the corridor outside. Someone's
coming this way!'

The two pigs looked around quickly for
a place to hide. There was no furniture to
crouch behind, so Pete got down on all fours

and crawled under the table. Brian joined
him.

They held their breath and listened
for the footsteps. Moments later, the door
opened and several bears came in. Stuck
underneath the table, Pete and Brian could
see nothing but bear legs, all in smart
business clothes.

The bear at the head of the table tapped
a furry foot impatiently. A gruff voice said,
'Hurry up and sit down, you lot. Time is
money, and I don't like anybody wasting
either.'

Pete knew that this must be the voice of
the boss, Mr Sweetie.

'Right then,' said Sweetie. 'What's happening with the business plan? Winnie – what's the situation in the city?'

Winnie replied, 'Phase One was a complete success. The entire population is still asleep, Mr Sweetie, allowing Sweetie Foods workers to collect all of the island's beehives and bring them to Bear Bottom Farm.'

Underneath the table, Pete gave Brian a wide-eyed look. Brian gave him a sleepy-eyed look back.

'Good!' answered Sweetie. 'In that case, I'd like you all to lift your honey pots and drink a toast – to the success of Sweetie Foods!'

'To the success of Sweetie Foods!' chorused the bears around the table. There was the sound of slurping honey.

'And what about the production of the New Formula honey?' said Sweetie. 'Rupert – speak to me.'

Rupert answered: 'The first batch of

New Formula honey will be bottled and on its way to our distribution centres by two o'clock, Mr Sweetie.'

There was a moment's ominous silence, then Sweetie growled, 'I said be ready by 1.58, didn't I, Rupert? That's two whole minutes you're wasting. Two minutes of MY time and, as we all know, time is money. What a bear-faced cheek! You're a disgrace to Sweetie Foods and you're a disgrace to the business world!'

'But, Mr Sweetie —'

'No excuses,' snapped Sweetie, pointing a claw. 'Rupert, you're fired!'

The next moment, Rupert slid out of his chair and on to the carpet. He was fast asleep!

Underneath the table, Pete was frantically piecing together all of the evidence – one of the bears had said that the entire population of Bear Island was sleeping. And then Rupert had drunk from his honey pot and he had fallen asleep. These two facts *must* be connected. Had Sweetie Foods somehow sent all of the island's bears to sleep? And if so, *why*?

Pete glanced at Brian, and saw to his horror that the medic had fallen asleep, too. Of course! Brian had gone and tasted the honey from the second vat! It had put him to sleep! This was terrible. It became even more terrible when Brian began to snore. Pete reached for the medic's snout in panic, but then he paused as he heard the bears around the table chuckle. They all thought that the snoring was coming from Rupert!

Pete sat back and tried to relax.

And that's when Rupert began to snore, too.

For a couple of seconds, the bears around the table continued their meeting. And then Mr Sweetie demanded, 'What's going on? Rupert can't snore in stereo!'

The next instant, several furry faces appeared beneath the table.

'There are two pigs here!' exclaimed one.

Mr Sweetie's face joined the others glaring at the pigs. 'Don't waste my time telling me things I already know!' he growled. 'Time is money!'

'Yes, Mr Sweetie,' said the bears.

Huge, furry paws pulled Pete out from under the table and set him in front of Mr Sweetie. It felt as if the bear's tiny eyes were drilling into him.

'I want to know what you and your little chum are doing in my boardroom?' said the bear. 'Speak.'

'We're here to put a stop to your little plan, Sweetie,' said Pete, adding, 'whatever it might be.'

A volcano of rage was building up inside Sweetie. 'Do you have any idea who you're talking to? I am the richest bear on Bear Island. And do you know why?'

Pete shrugged. 'Er, you were incredibly lucky?'

'Because I have always known what I want!' roared Sweetie. 'And what I want is *money*! Nothing in the world can beat cold, hard cash . . . dosh . . . readies . . . lots and lots of lovely honk to spend.' He brought his furry muzzle close to Pete. 'And do you know what I HATE?'

'Erm . . . karaoke?' guessed Pete. 'Cream crackers? You might have to give me a clue . . .'

'What I hate is anything that stops me from making *more* money,' growled Mr

Sweetie. 'Like you and your little friend
here, snooping around my honey factory.'

'OK, but how exactly do you intend to
make money from honey that puts people
to sleep?' challenged Pete. 'Tell me *that*,
Sweetie.'

'The honey we're going to sell isn't like
the strong stuff we gave Rupert or the
bears on the island,' Sweetie growled. 'It
contains just enough of the New Formula

to let animals relax and unwind from their stressful lives. It will make them feel calmer, more peaceful. If they have a spoonful before bed, it will help them drift off to sleep.'

Pete pointed at the honey pot in front of Sweetie. 'So has *your* honey got any of the New Formula in it?'

'Don't be silly!' scoffed Sweetie. 'We haven't done any studies to see if it's safe! That would have cost far too much!' He glanced at his expensive wristwatch and then turned to one of the bears around the table. 'We've wasted enough time on these pigs. Take them to the Research and Development department. Doctor Oswald can deal with them.'

It seemed to Pete that every bear around the table gave a little shudder at the mention of the name *Doctor Oswald*.

Still lying asleep on the floor, Brian let

out a low moan as if he was having a
nightmare.

'I know how you feel, Bri,' said Pete, as
the security bears dragged him away.

CHAPTER 7:

Piggylocks and the Three Bears

Once Curly had wiped his boots clean on the grass, he and Tammy continued along the trail through the woods, stepping more carefully now.

Finally the stretch of woodland ended and the pigs emerged into a different part of the city. There were houses here, as well as blocks of flats and one or two shops. But there were still no signs of life.

'What now?' asked Curly.

Tammy pointed to the little house directly across the road. 'That front door is part-way open. Maybe the cub is in there?'

When they reached the porch steps, the pigs slowly pushed the front door fully open. 'Hello?' called Curly. 'Anyone home?'

There was no answer.

Tammy wandered into the kitchen. 'Someone's been here recently,' she said. 'The stove's still warm.'

On the table sat three bowls of porridge. Curly shook his head in disbelief. 'Isn't

this weird?' he exclaimed. 'It's just like that fairy tale. You know the one – Piggylocks comes into a house and finds three bowls of porridge?'

Tammy stared blankly. 'How is that the same? There's two of us, and I haven't got blonde hair.' She picked up one of the bowls.

'What are you doing, Tammy?'

'I'm examining the evidence,' she said, grabbing a spoon. 'Plus . . . I'm a bit peckish.'

She shovelled a spoonful of porridge into her mouth.

'OWEE!' she cried, spitting it out. 'Too hot!'

She grabbed the second bowl. Moments later she was spitting that spoonful out, too. 'Ooh, yuck! This one's too *cold*!' she complained. 'The cook here's rubbish!'

Tammy moved on to the third bowl.

'Can't you see how this is just a *bit* like that old fairy tale?' asked Curly. 'I'll bet that third bowl tastes *just right*?'

Tammy chewed silently.

She chewed some more.

Then she cried, 'JUST RIGHT? Are you joking? It's the right temperature, but it tastes like wallpaper paste!'

She took another spoonful, then another.

'Erm, why are you still eating it, if it's so disgusting?' asked Curly.

'I'm a growing pig!' Tammy's spoon hovered in mid-air. 'But you're quite right.' She marched to the kitchen cupboard. 'I can make it a bit less disgusting, at least.'

She pulled out a jar from the cupboard and began spooning honey into the bowl.

'That should help,' she said. She was

about to tuck in again, when Curly looked to the window in alarm.

A sound had broken the silence outside. It was the motorbikes again – the Gruesome Grizzlies were back and they were coming this way!

The roar of the engines grew louder and louder, and then it stopped suddenly.

'They're parking outside the house!' cried Curly. 'Don't tell me they *live* here!'

'At the moment they can live in every house in the city!' said Tammy. 'They probably just decided to raid this one to make their food. We'd better get out of here!'

They ran out into the hallway. It was too late to leave through the front door now, but there were two other doorways at the end of the hall. Tammy dashed towards the far one, but fear froze Curly on the spot. He could hear heavy footsteps approaching outside. Any second now the door would open. He didn't even have time to make it to the door at the end of the hall! His mind in a whirl, Curly pulled open the nearer of the two doors.

Uh-OH.

It was just a hallway closet. But with no time to do anything else, he dashed into it, just as the front door opened and the footsteps clumped down the hallway towards the kitchen.

Pete was in a brightly lit laboratory.

A small koala bear in a white lab coat and round spectacles was studying him carefully. 'Welcome to the Research and Development department of Sweetie Foods,' said Dr Oswald. 'This is where we develop and test all of the company's honey-related products.'

Pete looked around for good escape routes.

'There is no point in trying to escape,' commented Dr Oswald matter-of-factly. He nodded towards the enormous grizzly that had carried Brian here, still fast asleep. 'Say hello to Bruno. He used to be a cage fighter before he worked for Mr Sweetie. Bruno might get cross if you try to run away. Am I correct, Bruno?'

The huge bear nodded and rolled his gigantic neck as if getting ready for action. 'I like fightin',' he said.

'Quite so,' said Dr Oswald. He poured some steaming liquid into two cups and offered one to Pete. 'Would you care for a hot chocolate, Mr Porker?'

Noticing the suspicious look in Pete's eyes, the koala added, 'I am drinking a cup myself so you needn't worry about any . . . nasty surprises.'

Seeing the koala drink, Pete did the same. 'I've got a question for you,' he said to the koala. 'What are you doing here on Bear Island, Oswald? You're not a bear, you're a koala. They're not *proper* bears, are they?'

This annoyed Oswald, though his voice remained calm. 'I'll tell you exactly what koalas are,' he seethed. 'They are world experts at sleeping. The average koala sleeps for eighteen hours a day.' The koala took his spectacles off and Pete saw how red and bleary his eyes were. 'I, on the other hand, am not the average koala. I am a poor sleeper. To be precise, I have not slept a wink in over four years. However, I have not been idle in that time. I have dedicated myself to the scientific study of sleep.'

Suddenly Pete understood. 'I get it! You developed something you can add to the honey that makes animals sleep! And you gave it to almost everyone on Bear Island?'

The koala nodded. 'Mr Sweetie wanted no interruptions as we put his business plan for the New Formula into action.' Oswald clapped his paws together to signal that the discussion was at an end. 'And now it is time for you to join your friend in a little nap.'

Pete looked down at his empty cup. His eyelids were feeling very heavy all of a sudden. 'You put something in my drink too, didn't you?' he snarled, fighting back a yawn. 'But you had the same drink as me!'

Dr Oswald smiled coldly. 'As I explained, *nothing* puts me to sleep, Mr Porker. You, on the other hand, have the good fortune to take part in a fascinating experiment. The honey in your drink did not contain the usual New Formula honey. Instead it has an experimental formula I've been working on – I like to call it the *Nightmare* Formula. Not only will it send you into a deep sleep, it will also give you the worst nightmares you have ever experienced.' The koala adjusted his spectacles. 'I would say *Sweet Dreams*, but I fear that would not be fitting.'

'Hurr, hurr,' chuckled Bruno from the back of the room.

'You rotten little marsupial!' Pete made a leap for the scientist, but the room was already spinning around him. He crashed to the floor and watched it spin some more until it whisked him off to sleep.

CHAPTER 8:

Sweet Dreams

Unaware of everything around him, Brian Trotter slept. And as he slept, he dreamed a terrible dream:

> He was in a place he knew well. It was the set of his favourite television quiz Ultimate Brainbox Challenge. For years Brian had wanted to be a contestant on this quiz, and now here he was! He felt a thrill of excitement.
>
> The quiz-master was at her podium with a stack of questions.
>
> 'Your time begins now,' she said. 'What is the capital of Pig Island?'

Everyone knew that Porkchopolis was the capital of Pig Island!

But when Brian opened his snout, he heard different words coming from his mouth: 'Is it ... cheese?'

'No ... In the field of inter-species rescue, what do the letters P, I, P stand for?'

Brian's mind was screaming, 'Pigs in Planes!' but his mouth said, 'Seven.'

The quiz-master frowned. 'Incorrect. What is TWO plus TWO?'

'Yes?'

With each wrong answer, Brian could hear the studio audience gasp.

'Your next question ... Who –'

A beeping noise indicated the end of the round.

'I've started so I'll finish,' said the quiz-master. 'Who are you?'

Brian froze. His brain felt as if it had

been whizzed up in a blender.

'I'm going to have to hurry you,' said the quiz-master.

Brian looked around for help. That's when he caught a glimpse of himself on a TV monitor. He was wearing a leather jacket and his mirror shades were pushed up on to his quiff hair-do.

In Brian's worst nightmare, he looked as cool as Pete, but he knew nothing about anything!

* * *

Meanwhile, Pete Porker slept. And as he slept, he too fell into a dark, dark dream:

Bright lights were shining into his eyes, and he had to squint. He reached into his pocket for his mirror shades, but they weren't there. Nerves stirred in his tummy like evil butterflies – Pete never felt fully at ease without his shades.

The angle of the lights changed, and he recognized where he was – the set of the most boring snoozefest ever on TV, Ultimate Brainbox Challenge. Worse still, he was a contestant on it!

From her podium, the quiz-master said, 'Start the timer now,' then she fired the first question at him:

'What's the fifteenth largest town on Crab Island?'

'Is that in terms of physical size or

population?' Pete fired back.

'Erm, I'm not sure,' said the quiz-master.

'For size it's Pincerton, for population it's Arthropod Garden City.'

'Correct,' said the quiz-master. 'What's 6,957 divided by 9.35?'

'Simple,' said Pete. '744.064 . . .'

'Yes!' said the quizmaster, unable to hide her surprise.

'I haven't finished yet,' smiled Pete. '. . . 171.'

On and on it went. The questions became harder and harder, but for each one Pete seemed to produce a correct answer from nowhere. The studio audience was ooh-ing and ahh-ing; they knew they might be witnessing the show's highest score ever.

'And now the final question in this

round,' said the quiz-master. 'Just who do you think you are?'

Pete felt himself smiling. 'I am, of course, a mix of genetic and environmental factors,' he began. 'My exact DNA sequence is ...'

He paused as he caught a glimpse of himself on a TV monitor screen. Something was wrong with his hair: instead of the usual glorious, much-sprayed quiff, it appeared to be arranged in some sort of ... could it be ... a side-parting?

But that wasn't even the worst thing. He was wearing a CARDIGAN.

Worse than that, it was a beige cardigan.

Worse still, a beige polyester cardigan with patches on the elbows and a crumpled tissue poking out of one sleeve!

It was a thing of horror, the uncoolest item ever, but Pete knew he'd seen it before somewhere. He'd seen it on Brian! Brian Trotter had a cardie just like this.

That's who Pete looked like, like BRIAN TROTTER, from the line of colour-coded pens in his top pocket to the sensible sandals and grey socks on his trotters.

Pete felt a scream building in his chest. He was just like Brian!

CHAPTER 9:

Biker Bears from Ma's

Curly pressed his snout against the crack in the closet door. From this angle he could glimpse part of the kitchen across the hallway. One tall skinny bear had his back to the door. Curly could read *BORN TO BE WILD* on his biker jacket.

He was looking down at the table. 'Someone's been eating my porridge,' he murmured at last.

A heavyset grizzly sat at the kitchen table. Her eyes were tiny in her huge shaggy face. She snorted, 'You always say that, Papa John.' Then she glanced at the bowl in front of her. 'Hold on ... Someone's been eating MY porridge.' She slammed a sledgehammer fist on to the table. '*Nobody eats Big Momma's porridge and gets away with it!*'

'What about yours, Babe?' asked the tall bear.

Curly wasn't able to catch the mumbled reply, but moments later Big Momma cried, 'What's that? Someone's been eating YOUR porridge, too?'

A terrible thought struck Curly. Maybe the bear called 'Babe' was the little bear cub he and Tammy had been looking for? Listening to the wet snuffling noise as all three bears gobbled down their porridge anyway, Curly eased the closet door open. Maybe if he took just a step closer he'd have a better view into the kitchen. He took one step, then another. He could see the two bears who had been speaking, but not the third. Then an immense shape moved into view – the one called Babe was a gigantic bear, more like a small mountain covered in fur. On top of his head he still wore the Viking helmet.

'Are you feeling OK, Babe?' asked Papa John. 'You don't look too well.'

Suddenly Big Momma lifted her nose into the air. 'I can smell something weird,' she announced. She sniffed again and, still unseen in the hallway, Curly remembered a lesson from school – bears have got a fantastic senses of smell.

'You're right,' agreed Papa John. 'What is that smell? Sweaty socks? Manure?'

Big Momma shook her shaggy head. 'I know . . . it's PIG!'

She pushed the table back and jumped to her feet. Curly knew there was no point trying to stay hidden now. He leapt out of the closet and raced down the hallway towards the front door.

'Get him!' shouted Papa John.

Both he and Big Momma started towards the door, but at that exact moment Babe swooned to the floor. With his massive body blocking the way out of the kitchen, Curly had the extra second or two he needed. He yanked the front door open.

As he flew down the steps, a welcome sight came into view. Tammy! The PiPs mechanic was pulling up alongside the kerb on a little scooter.

'I found it outside one of the shops!' the PiPs mechanic shouted. 'Hop on!'

Curly raced down the front path and squeezed on to the little bit of seat not occupied by Tammy's rear end. Tammy revved the little scooter's engine. Its high-pitched whine sounded like a mosquito trying to lift a barbell, but it took off at a reasonable speed.

Behind them they could hear the angry shouts of the grizzlies emerging from the house.

Curly tightened his grip on Tammy's shoulders. 'What did you do to the bears' motorbikes so they can't follow us?' he shouted.

'Er . . .' said Tammy.

Curly felt panic rising in him like an express lift zooming up to a floor marked Total Panic. 'WHAT?'

'That's a good idea about the motorbikes,' Tammy answered. 'Wish I'd thought of that.'

Behind them they heard two of the gigantic motorbikes roar into life. The chase was on. Of course, the bears' powerful motorbikes were much faster than one little scooter carrying two pigs. But Tammy was a skilled rider. She threw the scooter into tight corners, and weaved in and out of obstacles that the bulkier

motorbikes weren't able to pass. At one point she zipped up on to the pavement.

'I'm not sure this is legal!' cried Curly, holding on tight.

They whizzed around another corner and were greeted by a horrible sight – the rest of the Gruesome Grizzlies gang were zooming towards them from this direction. With bikers behind them and in front, they were trapped. Unless . . .

On the other side of the road was a park entrance with a set of metal bollards to stop motorized traffic. There was just enough space for the scooter, but the huge motorbikes would never fit.

Twisting the scooter's throttle back, Tammy headed straight for it. Any second now they would be safe.

'Wait!' cried Curly.

Tammy hit the brakes and skidded to a halt. Curly was pointing to a small figure squatting next to a parked car. It was the bear cub.

Behind them the motorbikes were roaring closer.

'Hey, kid!' shouted Tammy. 'Come here, quick!' She did her best to smile in a friendly way.

The little cub scrunched up his nose. The motorbikes behind the pigs had rounded the corner, too.

'Come on!' shouted Tammy.

The cub got to his feet, and looked at all the big scary motorbikes coming their way. Then he shouted, 'I don't talk to strangers!' and skipped away towards the bikers.

Tammy and Curly didn't know what to do. Should they try and grab the cub or should they just save their own bacon? It didn't matter anyway – it was too late now. The other group of bikers had cut them off. They began to ride around the pigs in a circle. The air was thick with the smell of oil.

Curly saw Big Momma reach down from her motorbike and sweep the cub up with one mighty arm.

That was too much for Curly: he couldn't leave an innocent little cub with these dangerous bikers. He hopped off the back of the scooter and marched over to Big Momma, a determined look on his face and his bottom lip stuck out full. All the bears killed their engines, aware that something was going down. The little pig pulled himself up to his full height and put on his most official voice. 'As a member of the Pigs in Planes international agency, I insist you release that bear cub immediately. If you co-operate, we'll let you all off with just a written warning *this time.*'

This was the funniest thing the biker bears had ever heard. As their guffaws echoed, the little cub turned and stuck his

tongue out at Curly. Then he gave Big
Momma a bear-hug. That's when Curly
realized – the cub didn't want to be rescued
from the bikers – he KNEW them!

'I think there may have been a
misunderstanding,' Curly began.

Big Momma glared. 'We understand all right,' she growled darkly. 'We found Little Barney all alone in the streets. He's one of our own now, and the Gruesome Grizzlies look after their own. So the question is – what are we going to do with you two little piggies?'

Curly gulped. He didn't like the idea of parting company with his head. He had always been quite attached to it, mostly by the neck.

CHAPTER 10:

The Other Highway Code

The Gruesome Grizzlies crowded around the two pigs.

'What shall we do with them, Big Momma?' asked one bear.

'Tow them behind the bikes?' suggested another.

'Pull their heads off?' suggested a third.

Big Momma frowned. 'We never actually *do* that, Algernon,' she said. 'It's just a rumour we like to spread.'

Tammy piped up. 'You *should* be helping us work out what's happened to all the other bears on the island! Why is everyone except you and this cub still hibernating?'

Big Momma snarled. 'We don't care what the rest of bear society does. We're outlaws. If everyone's still sleeping, that just means more open road for us.' She looked down at the pigs' flightsuits. 'And we don't like pigs in uniforms coming here and telling us what to do.' She turned to the bikers. 'Take 'em away. Drop 'em in a cave or something.'

'Wait!' cried Tammy, stepping forward. 'Under the Ancient Code of the Bikers, I demand the right to a Challenge.'

The biker bears found this even funnier than Curly's warning.

'Sorry, little piggy. The Ancient Code of the Bikers only applies to . . . bikers,' laughed Papa John. 'The clue is in the name.'

Without a word, Tammy unsnapped her cuffs and rolled one sleeve up. The tattoo on her upper arm showed a boar's skull with flames all around it. Underneath it said GO

HOG WILD!

'I used to ride with the Hogs on Hogs,' said Tammy. 'So I'll say it again. Under the Code, I challenge you to the most noble of all battles – Trial by *Food.*'

Big Momma snorted. 'You may have been a biker once, but you're still a puny little pig. And you're challenging me, the roughest, toughest bear on the island, to an EATING CONTEST?'

Her huge mouth split into a grin. 'You're on. And when you lose, you and your little piggy friend are going to be in big, *big* trouble.'

She began to shout orders at members of the gang, telling some to set up a table in the road and others to go and get the food. While this was going on, Curly sat nervously with Tammy.

'I . . . didn't know you knew so much about bikers,' he said.

'When I was little, my babysitter was a member of the biggest motorbike gang on Pig Island,' said the mechanic. 'The Hogs on Hogs.' She saw Curly's confusion. '*Hogs* is a nickname for big old motorbikes. That's why I don't know any lullabies or little kiddie songs. As a piglet I only ever learnt hard rock classics. I never had a teddy bear or a dolly – I used to carry around the carburettor from a vintage Pink Streak

1,000cc motorbike.' She looked over to where several bears were bringing trays of food for the contest. 'When I got older, I rode with the gang for a while. It's where I first got interested in engines.'

'But aren't biker gangs dangerous?'

Tammy shook her head. 'There are a few with bad reputations, but even they follow the Code of the Bikers.'

This reminded Curly of the upcoming contest.

'What are you going to do?' he asked. 'That Big Momma is four times as big as you! She's a GRIZZLY BEAR! They can eat massive amounts of grub!'

Tammy smiled heroically. 'Yeah, but you're forgetting something, Curly – I'm a bit peckish.'

Meanwhile Pete was still trapped in his nightmare.

The quiz questions kept coming at him and he knew every single answer, even the ones nobody ought to know. The studio audience of elderly pigs gasped in admiration at each new answer, and with each gasp he felt his Coolness Level drop further. If he carried on like this, he would enter the previously unknown territory of Negative Cool.

The quiz-master was still going strong: 'What is the Latin name for the plant Deadly Nightshade?'

'Atropa Belladonna,' Pete heard himself answer.

He paused, not even listening to the next question. There was something about that last one, something important. If only he could put his

trotter on it ... DEADLY Nightshade?
That didn't ring any bells. Deadly
NIGHTshade? Nope, that wasn't it
either.

Deadly NightSHADE. Pete felt his
heart go SPROING! at the word shade.
And yet ... it still wasn't quite right.
What it needed was an s on the end.

'Shades,' he said aloud.

The quiz-master hesitated. 'Erm,
no. I'm afraid "SHADES" is not
the chemical formula for calcium
carbonate ...'

She moved quickly to the next
question. 'What is the distance from
our planet to Jupiter and back again,
to the nearest centimetre?'

'Mirror shades,' said Pete, ignoring
the question. 'That's what I should be

wearing – mirror shades.' He looked at the studio set all around him. 'This is all just a bad dream. But it's MY dream, and that means I get to say what happens in it. And Pete Porker doesn't go anywhere without shades.'

He dipped a trotter into his pocket again. This time it closed around the familiar shiny plastic of his shades. Pete pulled them out and popped them on.

That was better! He might not be able to see all that well with his shades on, but he could certainly think better. And what he thought now was, I'm way too cool for a crummy nightmare like this.

As soon as he thought this, the cardigan disappeared in a puff of smoke.

He looked around at the TV studio.
I don't think much of this either,
he thought, and instantly everything
began to shimmer and change. Before
he knew it, he was standing on a sandy
beach. The studio audience of elderly
boars had become a group of fellow
sun-worshippers. Pete realized that
he himself was wearing nothing now
but his shades, his bright-red Speedio
trunks, and a gold chain with letters
that spelled out WHO DA PIG?

A breeze was blowing but Pete knew that not a single strand of hair was breaking rank from his quiff: that's what six bottles of gel and hairspray every day will do for you.

He smiled — all was well with the world again.

And now, he thought, it's time to wake . . .

Pete opened his eyes.

'. . . up!'

CHAPTER 11:

Battle of the Biker Bellies

Both eaters in the contest set off at a good pace. Big Momma favoured sweeping the food into her mouth with a swipe of her gigantic claws, while Tammy preferred to bend down and vacuum the food off the plate with her snout. In this way, they matched each other plate for plate. After each one was emptied, the eater would shout 'CLEAR!' and another loaded plate would be placed on the table.

The early rounds went fast – tottering stacks of pizzas disappeared, mountains of mashed potatoes vanished, industrial-sized

buckets of tomato soup were drained in
single guzzles.

With the bears all roaring for their leader,
Curly wanted to cheer his team-mate along,
too. He was just never quite sure what to
say at sporting events. He settled on, 'Chew
and swallow, chew and swallow . . . that's
it, Tammy, find your rhythm! Chew and
swallow, chew and . . .'

Tammy stopped eating for a moment and
just looked at him.

'Oh, er . . . come on, Tammy!' cried Curly,
deciding general encouragement might be
better.

On and on the two contestants ate. After
thirty minutes of relentless chomping, the
strain was beginning to show. Both eaters had
slowed down. Tammy had gone a worrying
shade of red, while Big Momma's little eyes
looked glassy and dazed. But neither gave in
– it was a matter of species honour now.

As they neared the hour mark, every bite,
every swallow, became an effort. Both bear
and pig looked ready to burst. As yet more
plates arrived, Tammy groaned and pushed
her chair back from the table. Crowding
around, all of the Gruesome Grizzlies held
their breath – this little pig had put up a

terrific fight, much better than anyone expected, but now she was about to admit defeat.

Tammy winced in pain. She rocked her head back and then . . .

'BLAAAAAAAAAAAAAAARRRP!'

She unleashed a volcanic burp.

The bears looked on in astonishment as Tammy patted her tummy and grinned. 'That's better!' she said brightly. 'Just needed to clear a little room.'

She started tucking in to the next plate of food with renewed energy.

This was too much for Big Momma. The gigantic grizzly slumped back. 'Enough,' she moaned. 'I can't eat another thing.' She looked at the pig with bleary eyes. 'You win. State your victory terms.'

Awake at last, Pete looked around. He was still lying in Oswald's laboratory. Feeling thick-headed from his nightmarish sleep, he sat up . . . and noticed that he was all alone. *Where was Brian?*

Pete rushed out into an empty corridor. His gut instinct told him to check out the main part of the factory, so he headed in that direction. As usual, his gut was correct – when Pete reached the factory floor, he spotted Brian. The PiPs medic was lying, still fast asleep and flat on his back, on one of the many machines in the room. His face was twitching and grimacing as if he was in the grip of a terrible nightmare.

There wasn't time to find out what, because there was someone else here – Dr Oswald. Still in his lab coat, the little koala was scurrying towards the exit on the other side of the factory floor.

'Stop right there, Ozzy!' shouted the PiPs captain.

The koala looked surprised to see Pete awake, but only for a second. 'Your nap ended earlier than expected,' he said. 'No matter.' A little smile played on his face.

'What's so funny?'

'You have a bear behind,' answered the koala.

'Yeah, right! I think I'd know it if I had a bare behind,' snorted Pete. He secretly reached a trotter round the back just to double-check there wasn't an unfortunate botty-displaying rip in his trousers.

Then he heard a low growl and looked round. It was a bear! *A bear behind* him! What's worse, it was Bruno the ex-cage-fighting grizzly, flexing his claws in preparation for action.

'And now if you'll excuse me,' said Dr Oswald. 'I cannot *bear* the sight of blood.'

'Me neither,' said Pete. 'Especially my own.'

Oswald left, but Pete hardly noticed. His full attention was taken by Bruno, who was bearing down on him with a mean-looking grin.

'Haven't you heard?' said Pete. 'Violence never solves anything.'

In answer, the grizzly slashed at Pete with his long, sharp talons. Pete leapt back just in time. 'Oi!' he cried. 'You want to give those claws a bit of a trim, mate. You could do someone a nasty injury.'

But Bruno wasn't the sort of bear who

worried about
health and safety
regulations too
much. 'Stay still,
pig, and fight
like a bear!' he
snarled, swinging
again.

'I'd rather fight
like a pig and
duck!' answered
Pete, and he did
duck, right
under the
bear's massive
shaggy arm. He
raced forward
on to one of
the factory
machines.

Bruno watched as the pig scrambled across it. 'You can't run forever,' he said darkly. He too climbed on to the piece of machinery and started to clamber across.

'Maybe I don't need to,' said Pete, looking back. He clicked a switch on the wall and the machine came to life. It was the big circular drum and it began to spin around at high speed.

'Enjoy the ride,' said Pete.

'WAAH!' replied Bruno, whooshing round and round in a high-velocity blur. He was only able to hold on for a few seconds at such speed, and then he shot off, slamming into the wall.

It was then Pete realized that the spinning drum wasn't the only machine on the factory floor that he had switched on. *All* of the automated machinery had come to life. Engines whirred and belts hummed, and Pete realized to his horror that Brian was lying on top of one of the now-moving conveyor belts.

It was carrying the PiPs medic right towards another machine – the one with the blade that usually chopped the beeswax off the honey frames. Only now it wasn't going to be a beeswax chopper.

It was going to be a bacon slicer.

Pete whirled around to turn the main switch off again. There was just one tiny problem, although in fact it wasn't very tiny at all: it was big. And *hairy*.

Bruno was back on his feet and blocking Pete's way to the switch. After slamming into the wall, he was as angry as a bear with a sore head. This was because he WAS a bear with a sore head.

And also some very sharp claws.

Meanwhile, on the other side of the

factory floor, Brian continued to trundle towards the whirring blades of the chopper. If Pete didn't do something fast, things were going to get very messy . . .

CHAPTER 12:

A Sticky End

The biker bears were all looking at Tammy with new-found respect. She had the right now to make any demands she wanted.

'I only want information,' Tammy told them. 'I want to know why your gang and Little Barney are the only ones who are still awake?'

Big Momma shrugged. 'We just thought everyone else was really tired.'

'Hold on,' piped up Curly. 'Not *all* of the Gruesome Grizzlies are still awake. That big one called Babe fell asleep back at the little cottage, after he ate his porridge.'

'He's still sleeping,' confirmed one of the bikers. 'I tried to wake him up.'

Tammy nibbled some more food to help her think. 'Perhaps it was the porridge?'

Big Momma shook her head. 'We ate the porridge, too, and we're OK.'

'Yes, but Babe was the only one who ate porridge with the honey Tammy put in it!' cried Curly. 'Maybe it was the *honey*!'

Big Momma pulled a face.

'What's wrong?' asked Tammy. 'Don't you like honey?'

Big Momma leaned forward. 'Do you know that bees throw it up? It's ACTUALLY bee vomit!'

Tammy started to get a feeling that they were on to something. 'What about the rest of the gang?'

Big Momma flexed her paws. 'My word is law to the Gruesome Grizzlies. And in this gang the rule is, *no honey*.' Several of the biker bears nodded in a way that made it clear they didn't like this rule very much.

Curly turned to Barney. 'What about you?' he asked the cub. 'Do you like honey?'

'Can't eat honey!' Barney shouted, even though he was less than a metre away. 'My mum says I'm *allergic* to it! She says it makes me . . .' He tried to remember the big word. '. . . *uncontrollable*.'

Curly turned to Tammy. 'Can you remember anything about the jar?'

The mechanic nodded slowly. 'Yes . . . it was from Bear Bottom Farm.'

'That's where Pete and Brian went!'

Tammy was already trying to call the other two on the radio, but there was no answer. 'We have to go there FAST!' she cried.

Big Momma got to her feet as quickly as she could, given the amount of food she had put away.

'Listen up, Gruesome Grizzlies!' she roared. 'Let's ride!'

Pete knew he'd never get past Bruno to reach the OFF switch.

He looked across the factory floor towards Brian. In a few seconds, the sleeping pig would reach the machine's blade. Could Pete get to his friend before Brian became nothing more than a pile of thinly sliced ham?

He had to try.

Sensing that the grizzly was hot on his trotters, Pete charged towards the two gigantic vats of honey that lay between him and Brian.

The one on the left was closest to the conveyor belt, but Pete ignored it and went for the vat on the right. He swan-dived into the honey with a great sticky SPLOOSH! and began to swim. Pete was a good piggy-paddler, but this was like swimming in slow-motion.

Behind him, Bruno charged towards the vats, too.

'Come here, pig!'

He leapt into the honey, too, but he chose the other vat. As the grizzly landed – SPLUSH! – a tidal wave of honey slopped out over the sides. Bruno knew he could

make it across with two strokes of his
enormous arms.

But then he began to slow down. He
let out a massive yawn and rolled around
in the honey so that his back was resting
against the side of the vat. Within a couple
of seconds, Bruno was fast asleep.

'Ha! Wrong vat, pal!' said Pete,
clambering out of the honey.

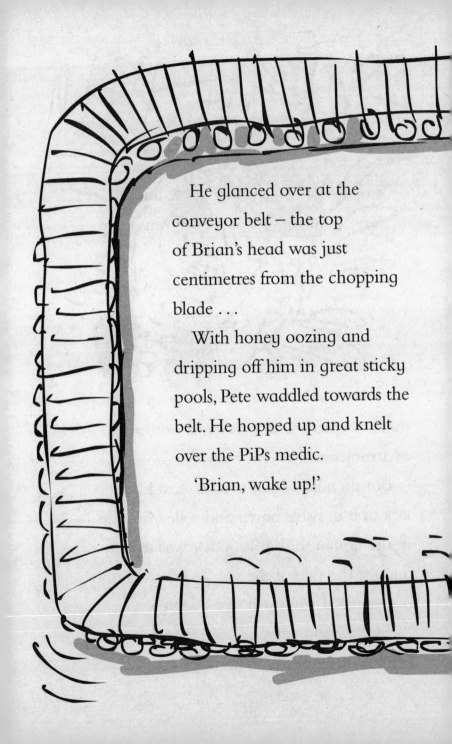

He glanced over at the conveyor belt – the top of Brian's head was just centimetres from the chopping blade . . .

With honey oozing and dripping off him in great sticky pools, Pete waddled towards the belt. He hopped up and knelt over the PiPs medic.

'Brian, wake up!'

The medic's eyes didn't open, but he began to murmur, 'Not stupid! I'm not stupid!'

Pete glanced up – they had almost reached the chopper. He could see its blade glinting, hear it swishing through the air. Pete wasn't sure how a noise could sound *sharp*, but this one managed it quite nicely.

'Sorry, Bri,' he said. He grabbed the medic's shoulders and then rolled off the conveyor belt on to the floor. The landing

didn't hurt too much, mainly because he landed on top of Brian.

'OW!' groaned the medic. His eyes fluttered open. What was going on? Why was he lying on the floor? Why was Pete staring down at him? And why did the captain look so very *sticky*?

He felt as if he still had one trotter in the awful world of his nightmare. 'I don't want to be cool and I don't want to be stupid,' he mumbled. He blinked and forced himself to focus on the captain's honey-covered face. 'I'm *not* stupid.'

'I know that.' Pete smiled. 'And I've got news, Bri . . . You're not cool either.'

He helped Brian to his trotters.

'So what happened to you?' the medic asked, pointing at the honey still dripping from Pete.

'Let's just say, I got into a bit of a sticky situation,' the captain replied with a grin.

'Get it? *Sticky?* Like honey?' His grin shrank. 'Don't you get it, Bri?'

'No,' said Brian, rubbing his eyes.

Pete pointed to the sleeping grizzly draped over the side of the vat. Bruno's nose was twitching and he was growling in his sleep.

'At least I was smart enough not to jump in the honey they've treated with special sleepy formula,' Pete said. 'The way I tricked him was sweet . . . You know, *sweet* . . . like honey? Tell me you get *that* one, Brian.'

'I get that one,' said Brian.

'Really?'

Brian shook his head. 'No, not really.'

Pete was about to have another go at explaining the joke but then he stopped. He was more a pig of action than a deep thinker, but a thought was tugging at him.

'Something's wrong here, Brian,' he said uncertainly.

'You've got that right,' boomed an angry voice from the other side of the factory floor. 'And as far as I can tell, you pigs are the cause of it.'

The PiPs turned to face a bear in an expensive suit striding angrily towards them.

Pete smiled. 'Hi, Sweetie.'

CHAPTER 13:

Killer Instinct

The Gruesome Grizzlies roared along the empty streets of Ursalona.

Big Momma led the way, and Tammy rode beside her. She had traded in her scooter for something with a bit more *oomph* – Babe's huge motorbike. Curly rode behind her, while Little Barney rode with Big Momma.

Curly had to admit, it was pretty exciting zooming along with his pink ears flapping in the wind and dozens of motorbikes roaring behind him.

'We're near Bear Bottom Honey Farm,'

Big Momma cried over her shoulder.

Up ahead they could see a metal gate
with a padlock on it. Tammy twisted the
throttle faster.

'What are you doing?' cried Curly.

'It's like that song of yours,' yelled Tammy.
'Can't go *round* it!'

'Can't go *under* it!' added Big Momma,

speeding up, too.

'Got to go THROUGH it!' they cried,
and they both pulled the huge motorbikes
up into wheelies. The front tyres hit the gate
together, blasting it clean off its hinges.

Now nothing lay between them and the
honey production plant.

★ ★ ★

Sweetie was striding furiously towards Pete and Brian. With one paw he reached for his ultra-thin mobile.

'Wait, Sweetie!' cried Pete. 'Before you make that call, I think you should know something.'

The businessbear ignored him and started punching in numbers.

'It might save you a lot of money.'

Sweetie hesitated. His eyes narrowed. 'You've got ten seconds to explain,' he grunted.

'Ten seconds?' spluttered Brian. 'I'm not sure that's long enough really . . .'

'Six seconds, five . . . four . . .'

Pete jumped in: 'You think all the trucks are full of honey with Oswald's New Formula, right? The one that just makes people drowsy? Well, think again. Those trucks are full of something much more powerful – Oswald's secret NIGHTMARE Formula!'

'Prove it,' Sweetie snarled.

'Oswald gave me some of his Nightmare Formula. It knocked me out and gave me the worst dream ever.' Pete pointed at Brian. 'But the same thing happened to my friend here . . . You had terrible dreams, too, didn't you, Brian?'

'Dreadful,' said Brian, not meeting Pete's eye.

'The thing is, Brian wasn't given any special Nightmare Formula in the lab. The only honey he tasted was from right here.'

Inside the vat, Bruno was growling in his sleep and frowning as he tossed his huge head from side to side.

'And just look at him!' continued Pete. 'He fell asleep as soon as he tasted the honey in there.'

'No, Mummy,' the sleeping bear mumbled. 'I *want* to be a cage fighter, I don't want to be a ballet teacher.'

'That sounds like a nightmare to me,' said Pete. 'You have to believe me – Oswald tricked you. He's put the Nightmare Formula into the main supply of honey!'

Sweetie was thinking hard. If his New Improved Honey gave animals everywhere terrible nightmares, that would be really bad. Not bad as in *wicked* . . . bad as in *bad for business*! Sweetie Foods would lose a lot of money; HE would lose lots of lovely money.

He jabbed a different number on his phone. 'Is that you, Oswald?' he growled. 'Get to the factory floor now. I've got some questions for you.'

'I'm afraid that won't be possible,' replied Oswald's voice on the speakerphone. 'I haven't got time.'

'TIME? Time is money!' roared Mr Sweetie. 'MY money!'

'There are more important things in

the world than money,' replied Oswald. 'For example, there is sweet, sweet revenge, and that is what I intend to have.'

Sweetie's eyes bulged. 'You're fired, Oswald!' he roared. 'Do you hear me? FIRED!'

But the line was already dead; Oswald had hung up.

Sweetie was frantically dialling a different number. 'Security?' he growled. 'Find Oswald and bring him to me.'

'Doctor Oswald has gone to the hangar to wait in your private jet,' replied the security guard. 'He said he was following your orders.'

'Do NOT let him near my plane!' screamed Sweetie into the phone. 'Go and get him NOW!'

'Um, I'm . . . not sure we can, sir,' replied the guard nervously. 'We've got a bit of a situation here, sir. A gang of bikers have broken through the outer fence and are heading this way. Here they are now, I –'

The rest of his words were drowned out by the roar of motorbike engines.

Sweetie clicked the phone off. He wasted three whole seconds staring in furious silence at the two pigs. Somehow this was scarier than all of his angry shouting. 'I'm a self-made bear,' he said at last, struggling to keep calm. 'I've succeeded in the business world because of my killer instinct. But a killer instinct isn't only good for business!'

'It probably also helps in competitive

sports,' said Brian helpfully.

'And ripping my enemies to shreds!' howled the bear. He tore off his silk tie, and charged wildly at the two pigs.

CHAPTER 14:

Everybody do the Brian (Again)!

The giant motorbikes of the Gruesome Grizzlies – plus one Hog on a Hog – roared towards the honey factory. Before they got too close, the lead bikes pulled up near a row of beehives. Big Momma lifted Barney gently to the ground.

'Curly, can you stay here and look after the cub?' asked Tammy.

The trainee PiP didn't really want to be a babysitter – he wanted to be in the action – but he knew that *the action* was no place for a young cub.

He watched glumly as the bikers zoomed

off. Barney didn't seem all that happy to be left out either. To cheer the young bear up, Curly said, 'Do you want to play a game of something?'

The cub scrunched up his snout in thought. 'We could play Poohsticks.'

Curly remembered that game from his childhood. 'But don't we need a stream and a couple of sticks to race?' he asked.

'Not the way I play,' said Barney. 'You find some poo, then you throw it at things and see if it sticks.'

'Ah,' said Curly. 'Perhaps we'll just wait here quietly.'

Meanwhile, the Gruesome Grizzlies had reached the loading area next to the factory. They found several bears in Sweetie Food uniforms loading crates of honey jars into the back of waiting trucks. Half the biker bears took off to stop the trucks that had already left; the rest stayed behind to make sure that none of the other trucks could leave.

The Sweetie Foods bears put their paws nervously into the air.

'We won't give you any trouble,' said the foreman.

'Really?' Big Momma sounded disappointed. 'Not even just a little bit?'

Over on the other side of the factory, Brian and Pete burst out of the exit, pursued by a bear in a business suit. Pete – much slower than usual in his honey-soaked flightsuit – hopped to one side and crouched behind a low wall. Meanwhile, Brian charged straight ahead towards the beehives. Not seeing the PiPs captain, Sweetie gave chase to Brian.

Pete just watched them go, knowing he was unable to catch up and help. He stood there for a moment, wondering what to do. He knew that Oswald was trying to escape in Sweetie's private jet, but didn't have a clue how to stop the mad little koala. He could hear the sound of motorbikes, but had no idea who the riders were or what they were doing. And then the sound of one engine grew louder, and a huge motorbike roared around the corner. It was Tammy! When she saw him, the PiPs mechanic skidded to a stop with a squeal of rubber on concrete.

She took one look at all the honey still taking its own sweet time to drip down from the captain. 'Looks like you've been in a sticky situation,' she said.

'I've already done that one,' Pete answered with dignity.

'Oh,' said Tammy. She revved the bike. 'Fancy a lift then, honey?'

Brian ran through the beehives as fast as his little trotters could carry him, but it was no good: Sweetie was gaining on him. He could hear the bear's growl getting closer and closer.

Brian realized that he couldn't outrun Sweetie, and he certainly couldn't beat him in a fight. What options did that leave?

Suddenly an idea buzzed into his head. He whirled around and began to do an odd little dance, moving his body in tight little circles followed by zig-zag diagonal steps.

Sweetie slowed down. 'Doing a stupid little dance isn't going to save you,' he growled.

Brian continued to do his odd moves. 'This "stupid little dance" is actually a re-creation of the dance bees do to tell the rest of their hive where nectar is,' he said. The noise of buzzing grew louder all around them.

'What I'm currently saying,' continued Brian, 'is that there is an excellent source of nectar nearby ... YOU!'

Sweetie just scoffed, but then the first of the bees shot towards him.

He swatted it away with one
paw. 'Get off!'

Soon another bee was flying at him,
then another. 'I said, go AWAY!' cried
Sweetie, a note of panic in his voice now.

The bees gathered together into a
low-flying black cloud and swarmed at
the businessbear. Sweetie turned and fled.

'You're FIRED!' he roared over
his shoulder. But not appearing to
understand that they were employees
of Sweetie Foods, the bees flew on.

CHAPTER 15:

King Bee

In another section of the beehives, Curly just stood and wondered what exactly was going on. He had seen several of the Gruesome Grizzly bikers zooming after some trucks and he had heard what sounded like a jet engine firing up. Meanwhile, here he was, stuck babysitting a bear cub.

'Don't worry,' he said for the umpteenth time. 'It'll all be OK.'

There was no answer from Barney.

'Did you hear me, Barney?'

Still no answer.

Curly looked around. 'Barney!'

The annoying little cub had wandered off! Once again he had dropped his battered old teddy bear on the ground and scarpered.

Curly grabbed it and ran among the hives to find the runaway cub before he got himself into trouble.

Meanwhile Dr Oswald had made his way to the hangar and was sitting in the cockpit of Sweetie's private jet, engines idling and all systems go. As soon as he reached the runway, he would blast away from here.

The radio on the console crackled into life. 'Why did you do it, Oswald?' cried the voice of Peter Porker.

Oswald picked up the microphone. 'How else could I have my revenge?'

'Revenge on WHO?'

'On everyone who is able to get a good night's sleep!' cried the koala, still taxiing the plane out of the hangar. 'Can you imagine how it is for those of us who *can't* sleep? Sitting wide awake while all around drift off to blissful bye-byes? Listening to them snore, all tucked up in bed in their stupid pyjamas and nightgowns? Watching them drool, while I myself am unable to get a wink of sleep?'

The plane had reached the start of the runway now. Oswald fired up the engines for take-off. The jet began to race forward.

As he picked up speed, he became aware of something else up ahead. Off to one side, there was a motorbike, and it was zooming towards the runway. It looked as if a pig was riding it, and on the back sat a strange honey-coloured creature. It appeared to be holding a radio transmitter.

Of course, this was Peter Porker! Sitting in front of him, Tammy pulled her trotter back on the throttle and gave it all she'd got – the motorbike shot forward like a two-wheeled rocket.

Tammy had spotted something next to the runway – a small construction site where Sweetie Foods had laid the foundations for a new building. There was a plank of wood leaning up against a mound of sand. It was the perfect motorbike jump ramp! Tammy gunned the motorbike. Its engine screamed. The sound of that engine mingled with the roar of the jet.

Tammy timed it perfectly, hitting the ramp just as the jet reached this part of the runway. The bike whizzed up and then soared into the air.

At first it looked like they would smack right into the nose of the plane, but the bike had enough speed and lift to carry it right over the top of it. At the highest point, Pete realized what he had to do. He rolled to one side and dropped off the motorbike seat.

He landed right on the front window of the speeding plane, where his coating of honey helped him stick with a squelch.

Looking like the world's worst window cleaner, Pete tapped on the thickened glass and shouted, 'Stop the plane!'

Inside the cockpit, Oswald did not slow the plane down – he just leaned to one side so he could see past the pig on his windscreen. The plane was still picking up speed for take-off. Pete's eyes grew wide as he began to slide down off the window.

This wasn't good . . .

Meanwhile Curly had caught up with Barney, the runaway bear cub.

'What did you think you were doing?' the trainee PiP demanded. 'Didn't I tell you to stay with me?'

The little bear just shrugged. 'Dunno.'

'Here,' said Curly with a sigh. He held out the battered old teddy bear. 'You dropped this *again*.'

Barney looked at the stuffed toy with

disgust. 'I don't WANT that smelly old toy!'
he cried. 'Big Momma got it for me from a
charity shop! I keep throwing it away and
you keep on bringing it back to me. I want
a computer game, not a silly old stuffed toy!'

Curly wasn't sure what to say to that.
Luckily he didn't have to say anything
because:

1) The sound of the small jet approaching
along the runway made conversation
difficult.

2) A strange figure in a business suit
crashed through the beehives near them,
screaming at the top of his lungs. It was Mr
Sweetie, and he was screaming because a
gigantic cloud of bees was chasing him.

Sweetie looked up to see his own plane
approaching down the runway. As he did
this, he stumbled and went sprawling on
to the ground, right in front of Curly and
Barney.

The cloud of bees caught up with him immediately, but they did not stop at Sweetie. They had seen something even better; the bees zoomed towards the on-coming jet.

It was clear what they were aiming for – Pete. Thousands of bees descended on the honey-drenched pig, swarming all over the plane's honey-smeared windscreen, too, and covering every centimetre of the glass.

Now Oswald was unable to see anything at all. The plane swerved blindly off the runway. It trundled across the rough terrain, smashing wooden hives out of the

way, before coming to a stop right in front
of Curly, the bear cub and Sweetie. Pete
fell to the ground, still covered from head
to trotter in bees.

'Are you OK?' cried Curly.

'I'm fine,' answered Pete above the sound
of buzzing. 'They're not stinging me at all.
They must think I'm the King Bee!'

Sweetie was looking at the bee-covered
pig as if his own worst nightmare had
come to life. He held out his paws to Curly.

'I give up,' he cried. 'Just keep that giant
bee thing away from me!'

While the PiPs were arresting Sweetie,

none of them noticed the plane door open and Oswald stagger out. Quickly assessing the situation, the koala began to scamper away.

Then he spotted something and stopped.

He rubbed his red-rimmed eyes and edged towards Barney.

'Can . . . can I see that teddy bear?' he asked in a trembling voice.

'You can have it,' said Barney, throwing the battered old bear to the scientist.

Oswald caught it in both paws and stared in red-eyed disbelief. In his mind stirred a childhood memory of a young koala mislaying his favourite stuffed toy; of a young cub unable to get to sleep at bedtime because he couldn't stop thinking and thinking about that toy.

'Snooky-Ookums, after all these years, is it really you?' His voice choked with emotion. 'I thought I'd lost you forever.'

Oswald hugged the teddy to his lab coat. Then, ignoring the stares of the pigs and the furious buzzing of the bees and the roar of the motorbikes, he curled up on the ground and fell fast asleep for the first time in years.

EPILOGUE

It was all over. The bikers had rounded up all of the Sweetie Foods workers. One of the Gruesome Grizzlies had gone to the city and woken up the main population of Ursalona. The Bear Island police had eventually arrived, yawning, and bundled Sweetie and the sleeping Oswald into Panda cars.

The PiPs began to say their farewells. Curly was relieved to hand young Barney back to his parents, who had been brought out to Bear Bottom Farm by the police. Reluctantly the bees had flown away from

Pete back to their hives. The PiPs went to say their goodbyes to Big Momma and the Gruesome Grizzlies.

'There's one thing I don't understand,' Curly said. 'If Barney didn't make the emergency call, then who did?'

Babe, still looking sleepy because he'd only recently woken up, leaned towards Big Momma and whispered something.

'Babe's a little shy,' said Big Momma, 'but he wants me to tell you that *he* made the call.'

The immense bear in the Viking helmet nodded and gave a sweet little smile.

Big Momma was clapping Tammy on the back. 'Anyway, that was a great motorbike jump,' the leader of the biker gang said. 'You should come back to Bear Island, Tammy. We could get lunch together.'

Tammy thought this over. 'To be honest, all this excitement has given me a bit of an appetite right now. How about we grab a pizza or two before I fly back?'

And so, only a couple of hours after their legendary eating contest, the two headed off to get some grub.

That evening there were no emergency calls and so, for once, the Pigs in Planes had a quiet evening in back on Snout Island.

Curly wanted to show Tammy his favourite book from when he was little, *101 Songs and Rhymes for Little Piglets.* In

return she taught him the secret bikers'
oath and special handshake, in case he
ever ran into the Hogs on Hogs.

Pete bumped into Lola in the corridor
outside the Common Room.

'Where's Peregrine?' he asked.

'In there with Brian. Bri's just telling
him about communication in social
insects.' Lola rolled her eyes.

The captain went in and found the
medic and the Wing Commander in the
comfy chairs in front of the fire. Brian was
relaxing in his beige cardigan and telling
Peregrine all about the bees.

'It's really quite interesting, actually,
how they can give precise information
just by dancing.' Brian glanced at the
Wing Commander. 'Isn't that interesting,
Peregrine? . . . Peregrine?'

The Wing Commander's eyes were
open, but his head lolled forward and

a rumbling snore escaped from him.
Peregrine was asleep.

'My explanation of the life cycle of
social insects wasn't *so* boring, was it?'
asked Brian anxiously.

'Course not, Bri,' Pete said. 'It's just that
. . . Lola gave Peregrine a spoonful of the
proper New Formula honey in his warm
milk, that's all.'

The captain glanced at the door where
Lola was shaking her head to indicate
that she had done no such thing, but Pete
figured that the medic didn't need to know
this.

The two pigs looked into the fire for
a few minutes. Although neither of them
spoke, they each knew what the other was
thinking about. At last, Brian said,

'So, Peter . . . can you remember the
nightmare you had?'

'Crikey, yes!' said Pete. 'It was horrible!'

He paused, looking at his friend's eager little face in the glow of the firelight. How could he say that his nightmare had involved becoming a pig very much like Brian? 'I . . . I was being chased by these monsters who wanted to nick my shades. What about you, Bri? What did you dream about?'

Brian bit his lip. How could he say that his nightmare had involved becoming a cool pig not completely unlike Pete?

'Er, yes, well . . . I dreamed I was at the supermarket wearing nothing but a tiny pair of pants. It was terrible.'

'Doesn't sound too bad to me,' said Pete with a shrug. 'Takes all sorts, I guess.'

He clapped his friend on one shoulder and smiled. 'Anyway, Bri, I'd love to hear you explain some more about bee communication, or whatever. That would be . . . quite interesting, actually.'

'OK, Pete, but first . . .' Brian pointed a
trotter at Lola who was coming in with
a selection of hats in her arms. 'Let's just
see Lola balance that tiny cowboy hat on
Peregrine's head!'

READ MORE OINKCREDIBLY FUNNY ADVENTURES OF THE

Crossword

Across→

2. Tammy's word for a big old motorbike.

5. The Gruesome _____ .

7. What Dr Oswald needed to help him sleep.

8. Bear _____ Farm.

9. What bears do in winter.

11. The name of the bear cub who doesn't go to sleep.

Down ↓

1. Dr Oswald is one of these.

3. The capital of Bear Island.

4. In their nightmares Pete and Brian compete in Ultimate _____ Challenge.

6. The evil bear.

9. This food made all the bears fall asleep.

10. The challenge between Tammy and Big Mamma.

★ Turn to page 166 for the answers.

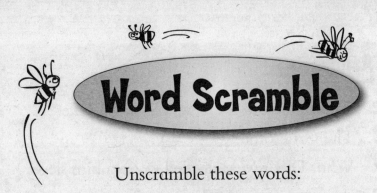

Word Scramble

Unscramble these words:

1. **HMCEiNCA**

2. **PEERBEKEE**

3. **ANSiLD**

4. **WSOADL**

5. **iOBTOKERM**

6. **LSAEPE**

7. **NASSLSSEGU**

8. **RUBON**

9. **ARGACIDN**

10. **MYTMA**

★ Turn to page 166 for the answers.

Wordsearch

Find the words opposite hidden in this grid.
(Look carefully – some may be
backwards or diagonal!)

G	A	P	O	R	R	I	D	G	E	Z	P
Q	R	E	T	O	O	C	S	M	R	O	F
O	Y	T	S	B	W	V	A	Q	R	Z	N
J	L	P	M	I	T	Q	C	K	Q	I	F
Y	L	R	U	C	A	D	C	K	G	H	Q
B	I	K	E	R	D	H	V	H	A	O	D
X	S	K	Y	H	O	G	T	P	J	N	B
C	I	E	D	P	T	M	O	H	C	E	Q
H	R	V	O	U	A	R	E	H	O	Y	O
K	B	L	S	R	K	D	O	P	A	M	T
A	I	N	E	E	E	D	Z	Z	F	C	A
S	G	T	R	O	E	V	I	H	E	E	B

★ Turn to page 166 for the answers.

BEEHiVE	PORKCHOPOLiS
BiKER	PORKER
CURLY	PORRiDGE
HONEY	SCOOTER
NiGHTMARE	SKYHOG

It all started with a Scarecrow.

Puffin is seventy years old.
Sounds ancient, doesn't it? But Puffin has never been
so lively. We're always on the lookout for the next big
idea, which is how it began all those years ago.

Penguin Books was a big idea from the mind of
a man called Allen Lane, who in 1935 invented
the quality paperback and changed the world.
**And from great Penguins, great Puffins grew,
changing the face of children's books forever.**

The first four Puffin Picture Books were hatched in 1940 and the
first Puffin story book featured a man with broomstick arms called
Worzel Gummidge. In 1967 Kaye Webb, Puffin Editor, started the
Puffin Club, promising to **'make children into readers'**.
She kept that promise and over 200,000 children became
devoted Puffineers through their quarterly instalments of
Puffin Post, which is now back for a new generation.

Many years from now, we hope you'll look back and
remember Puffin with a smile. **No matter what your age
or what you're into, there's a Puffin for everyone.**
The possibilities are endless, but one thing is for sure:
whether it's a picture book or a paperback, a sticker book
or a hardback, **if it's got that little Puffin
on it – it's bound to be good.**

Answers

Crossword

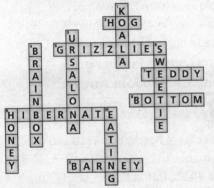

Wordsearch

G	A	P	O	R	R	I	D	G	E	Z	P
Q	R	E	T	O	O	C	S	M	R	O	F
O	Y	T	S	B	W	V	A	Q	R	Z	N
J	L	P	M	I	T	Q	C	K	Q	I	F
Y	L	R	U	C	A	D	C	K	G	H	Q
B	I	K	E	R	D	H	V	H	A	O	D
X	S	K	Y	H	O	G	T	P	J	N	B
C	I	E	D	P	T	M	O	H	C	E	Q
H	R	V	O	U	A	R	E	H	O	Y	O
K	B	L	S	R	K	D	O	P	A	M	T
A	I	N	E	E	E	D	Z	Z	F	C	A
S	G	T	R	O	E	V	I	H	E	E	B

Word Scramble

1. MECHANIC
2. BEEKEEPER
3. ISLAND
4. OSWALD
5. MOTORBIKE

6. ASLEEP
7. SUNGLASSES
8. BRUNO
9. CARDIGAN
10. TAMMY